To my husband, Lew, with deep gratitude for his unwavering love and support, and especially to Kayla and Olivia, who are the inspiration for this story.

www.mascotbooks.com

I Hug You in My Heart

For more information, please contact:
Mascot Books
620 Herndon Parkway, Suite 320
Herndon, VA 20170
info@mascotbooks.com

Library of Congress Control Number: 2020918720

CPSIA Code: PRT1120A
ISBN-13: 978-1-64543-746-8

Printed in the United States

April Goff Brown

Illustrated by Jeanne Conway

I Hug You in My Heart

It was a sunny Saturday morning, and Zoe was beyond happy. She was in the car on her way to visit her Nana for the first time in weeks. It was going to be a long ride, and Zoe spent the time thinking about the perfect weekend she would have with Nana making cookies, doing crafts, playing outside, snuggling up on the couch, and getting lots and lots of hugs.

As they neared Nana's street, Zoe said, "Turn right here!"

Her parents laughed, because Zoe said this every time she went for a visit. Zoe counted the houses until finally, there it was.

Zoe's favorite place in the whole world.

Zoe jumped out of the car, grabbed her bag, and ran to the front door. She opened it wide and shouted "Nana! I'm here!"

Nana appeared right away and gave Zoe the biggest hug ever.

"I am so happy you're here, Zoe!" Nana said.
"I have lots of fun things planned for us."

Zoe laughed, because Nana always said that.

"Yippee! Can we walk in the garden first?" Zoe asked. Walking in Nana's flower garden was one of Zoe's favorite things. She loved smelling all the pretty flowers, and she loved it even more when Nana let her pick some flowers to bring inside.

After Zoe found the perfect vase for her flowers,
she hoped that Nana would want to bake cookies.

"How about we bake some cookies?" Nana asked her.
"Yippee!" Zoe exclaimed.

Zoe loved making—and eating—cookies with Nana.
Nana always let her hop up onto the counter to help.

Once the cookies were made, Zoe knew what would be next. Nana would give her at least two fresh, warm cookies with a nice cold glass of milk for a snack.

"Nana," Zoe said as she took big bites and chewed the warm cookie, "these are the best cookies ever."

Nana just smiled. Zoe always said that.

BIRD HOUSES TO PAINT

After they tidied up the kitchen, Nana turned to Zoe. "Now that everything is clean, what do you think about going to the craft store?" Nana asked.

"Yippee!" Zoe cried. She had been hoping Nana would ask her that.

At the craft store, Zoe roamed the aisles, looking at everything until she could decide what she wanted to make.

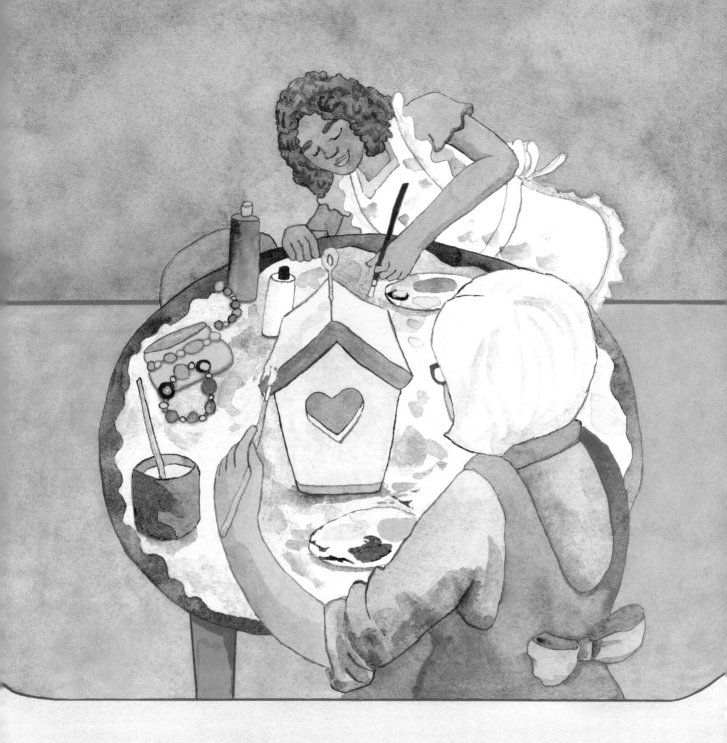

After they paid for all their goodies, Zoe and Nana returned home and spent the rest of the morning painting bird houses and making bracelets.

Before she knew it, her tummy was rumbling, and they stopped working to have some lunch.

After lunch, Zoe wondered what they would do next. Zoe was hoping that Nana would take her to the park to play.

"I was thinking," Nana said, "that this is a perfect day to go to the park. What do you think?"

"Yippee!" Zoe cried.

Zoe could not believe her good luck. This was turning out to be a perfect day.

Later that evening, after dinner, Zoe snuggled up on the couch with Nana to watch their favorite movie. Before long, Zoe let out a big yawn.

"Looks like someone is ready for bed," Nana said.

Zoe went upstairs, brushed her teeth and washed her face, and then got into her nice warm bed. Nana came into her room and tucked her under her favorite quilt that Nana made for her. Zoe was hoping Nana would sing her songs before she went to sleep. Zoe loved it when Nana sang her songs.

"Which songs would you like tonight?" Nana asked.
"We can do three."

Yippee, Zoe thought with another yawn. She told Nana the names of the three songs she wanted.

Then, she curled up on her pillow, with her quilt tucked under her chin, and listened while Nana sang her favorite songs, softly and quietly, while gently running her fingers through her hair. This made Zoe very, very sleepy, and soon, she was sound asleep.

The next day, Zoe had just as much fun as she did the day before. Nana made pancakes and bacon for breakfast. They worked in the garden, did more crafts, ate more cookies, and played games.

Before she knew it, it was four o'clock, and Zoe knew her parents would be coming to take her home soon. She knew it would be a long time before she would be able to visit again. This made Zoe feel very sad, and she started to cry.

"What's the matter, honey?" Nana asked. "Why are you so sad?"

"Nana, do you ever forget me when I'm not here?"
Zoe asked through her tears.

"Oh honey," Nana said as she pulled Zoe close to her in a warm, comforting hug. "I could never, ever forget you. I love you so much and you are always right here, in my heart," Nana said as she pointed to her chest. "Let me show you."

Nana pointed to the photographs of Zoe on the table.

"Every time I look at your beautiful face and those big brown eyes and that curly head of hair, I hug you in my heart," Nana said.

They went outside into the garden.

"Every time I come into my garden, I think of how much you love to be here, and I hug you in my heart," Nana said.

They went back into the house and went into the kitchen.

"Every time I make cookies, I smell their delicious aroma and I think how much you love my cookies, and I hug you in my heart," Nana said.

She pointed to the shelf where Zoe's crafts were on display.

"Every time I see your projects, I think of how creative you are, and I hug you in my heart," Nana said.

They went into the living room and sat on the couch.

"Every time I sit here and cuddle under my quilt when I watch TV, I remember how much you love to snuggle, and I hug you in my heart," Nana said to Zoe.

They went up into the bedroom.

"Every time I come in here, I remember how much you like me to sing you to sleep, and I hug you in my heart," Nana said.

"So, you see honey, I could never forget you. You have a special place deep inside my heart, and when I miss you, I just hug you tighter." With that, Nana gave Zoe a big, warm, loving hug.

"Let me ask you something, Zoe," Nana said. "Do you forget me when you're not here?"

Zoe thought for a second, and said, "Oh no, Nana. I could never forget you. I love you too much to forget you."

Right then, Zoe knew that her Nana would never forget her, even though they wouldn't see each other as much as they were used to.

Still, Zoe felt a little sad. Then suddenly, a great idea popped into her head.

"I know what we can do, Nana," Zoe said. "Let's make hearts, one for you and one for me, and we can put our pictures on them. This way, I can have you in my heart and you can have me in your heart."

"What a fabulous idea!" Nana said to Zoe.

They spent the rest of their day making and decorating hearts and taking their pictures to put on the hearts. When they were done, Zoe's parents came to get her.

Even though Zoe knew it could be a long time before she would see her Nana again, she was so happy to take the heart with Nana's picture on it home with her.

As Zoe got ready to leave, she turned to her Nana and said, "I love you so much, Nana. Can I have one more hug to take with me?"

Nana laughed and wrapped her up in her arms with the biggest, safest, warmest hug ever. It was the kind of hug that Zoe could keep with her deep inside her heart for a long, long time.

The
End

April Goff Brown retired in 2017 from a 35-year career of developing and managing youth programs, and she now relishes this stage of her journey as a creative entrepreneur and author. April is happily married to her husband of 40 years and is a proud mother to her son Jason, stepmother to April, mother-in-law to Cori, and Nana to ten. When not writing, she tends to her jewelry business, practices yoga, gardens, quilts, and assists with the virtual education of her youngest granddaughter, Olivia. April is a contributing author in *The Great Pause: Blessings and Wisdom from COVID-19*. This is her first children's book.